# Esme
## the Ice Cream Fairy

To all ice cream lovers everywhere

Special thanks to Sue Mongredien

ISBN 978-0-545-62239-4

# Esme
## the Ice Cream Fairy

by Daisy Meadows

SCHOLASTIC INC.

The Fairyland Palace

Candy Land

Goblins' ice cream truck

Market booth:

Charlie's ice cream truck

Kirsty's House

Wetherbury Village

I have a plan to make a mess
And cause the fairies much distress.
I'm going to take their charms away
And make my dreams come true today!

I'll build a castle made of sweets,
And ruin the fairies' silly treats.
I just don't care how much they whine,
Their cakes and candies will be mine!

# Contents

# Ice Cream Emergency

"Bye, Aunt Helen," said Kirsty Tate, hugging her aunt. "It was really nice to see you again."

"Thanks for all the candy," added Rachel Walker, Kirsty's best friend. She was staying with Kirsty over spring break.

Aunt Helen smiled at them. "My

pleasure," she said. "I'm sorry they weren't as good as usual, though."

Kirsty's aunt had the best job in the world: She worked at Candy Land, the treat factory just outside of Wetherbury. She'd come to have lunch with the Tates that day, bringing a big bag of Candy Land goodies for everyone. Unfortunately, the candy had tasted terrible. Something had gone horribly wrong!

The girls were disappointed—but their dismay had quickly turned to excitement when their friend Honey the Candy Fairy magically appeared in Kirsty's bedroom. She told them that strange things had been happening at her Fairyland Candy Factory, and asked if they'd help her.

Kirsty and Rachel hadn't hesitated for a second. Of course they'd help—they loved going to Fairyland! And so they'd been swept up in another wonderful fairy adventure, this time with Honey and her team of Sugar and Spice Fairies. It had been the most perfect start to the week, Rachel thought, smiling to herself.

The girls, Aunt Helen, and Kirsty's mom were now standing outside Tracy Twist's candy shop in Wetherbury, where Aunt Helen was catching the bus back to work. "I hope everything's working the way it should at Candy Land again," she said. "At least the lollipops were good."

"The lollipops were *delicious*," Kirsty replied, with a secret wink at Rachel. Earlier that day, the two of them had met Lisa the Lollipop Fairy. They had a thrilling time tracking down her magic lollipop charm, which had been stolen by wicked Jack Frost. Lisa used her magic charm to make lollipops everywhere lickable, and while it was missing they had tasted horrible. Luckily, Kirsty and Rachel had helped Lisa get it back. Now all the lollipops were yummier than ever!

"Good," Aunt Helen said. "I left a

special surprise for you back at your
house, which I hope you like, too." She
grinned at the girls. "Ah, here comes my
bus. Good-bye, all of you. Thanks for a
lovely lunch!"

"Bye!"
chorused
Kirsty, Rachel,
and Mrs. Tate,
waving to Aunt
Helen as the bus
drove away
slowly.

"I wonder what the
surprise is," Kirsty said
once the bus was out of sight.

"Knowing Aunt Helen, it's something
really good," Mrs. Tate said with a
smile.

Rachel smiled, too, and felt a fluttery feeling inside at the thought of a surprise waiting for them. Whenever she and Kirsty got together, life was always full of surprises!

They headed back toward Kirsty's house. As they walked through the market square, Rachel found herself looking out for more fairies. Honey had a team of seven Sugar and Spice Fairies, who helped her create delicious treats using their special magic charms. Unfortunately, Jack Frost had decided that he wanted all their yummy treats for himself. He was planning to

build a gigantic Candy Castle! He had
ordered his goblins to steal the magic
charms so he could make the best treats
ever. Unfortunately, while the charms
were away from their fairy owners,
candy and treats didn't look or taste as
good as usual!

Even worse, this had all happened just
before the fairies' annual Treat Day!
This was the day when Queen Titania
and King Oberon gave every fairy a
basket full of treats as a special thank-
you for their hard work all year. It
looked like those baskets would remain
empty—unless the girls could help the
Sugar and Spice Fairies get their magic
charms back from the goblins.

Kirsty was scanning the market booths
closely, too. "Mom, could we look

around a little, please?"
she asked. "We can
meet you at home
later, if that's
okay." The Tates
only lived a few
streets away, and
it was a safe walk
back.

"That's fine,"
Mrs. Tate said with a smile,
and took her wallet out of her
purse. "Here," she went on. "Let me give
you some spending money, just in case
you see something you like."

"Thank you!" Rachel said.

"We'll be back in an hour," Kirsty
promised.

The girls said good-bye and made their

way through the square. It was lined
with all kinds of booths, selling
jewelery, toys, local vegetables, and
brightly colored candles. Then they
spotted an ice cream truck, and Kirsty
licked her lips. It was a sunny day, and
she could really go for a delicious, cool
ice cream cone.

"They look good," Rachel said,
studying the sign propped up near the
truck. "Caramel Crunch—*mmm*, my
favorite."

"Chocolate Swirl sounds yummy, too," Kirsty said, her tummy rumbling. "Ooh, and Mint Chocolate Chip. How will we decide?"

The man in the truck smiled. He was wearing a white uniform and hat, and had a name tag with CHARLIE printed on it. "Would you like to try a few flavors?" he asked. "It might help you make up your minds."

"Yes, please!" both girls replied.

"No problem," Charlie said. He gave them each a tiny spoonful of Strawberries and Cream, then another of Mint Chocolate Chip.

Rachel put the pink strawberry ice cream in her mouth, expecting it to dissolve deliciously on her tongue. Instead, it felt like a flavorless lump of ice. "Oh!" she said in surprise.

Kirsty was about to try the Mint Chocolate Chip, but before she had even put the spoon to her lips, the ice cream melted to liquid and dripped onto the ground. Strange!

A horrible thought occurred to both girls at the same time. "This must be because of Jack Frost!" Kirsty whispered. "He's even ruining ice cream!"

# Enter Esme!

Another customer approached the ice cream truck and began giving Charlie a long, complicated order. Kirsty and Rachel seized the chance to slip away for a minute.

"Let's look around the truck," Rachel suggested in a low voice. "We might find another one of the Sugar and Spice Fairies."

"Good idea!" Kirsty agreed, feeling a flutter of excitement at the thought. Two fairy adventures in the same day would be a real treat!

The girls searched eagerly around the truck, hoping to see a sparkle, which would mean that a fairy was nearby. But even though they looked at every part of the truck, from top to bottom and front to back, they spotted nothing unusual.

They wandered around the front of the
truck again, where the customer was just
leaving. Her hands were full of ice cream
cones, none of which looked very tasty.

"Goodness!" Charlie exclaimed. "That
lady cleaned me right out of Chocolate
Chunk. Give me a minute, girls. I'll just
pop into the back to get some more."

Charlie vanished into the back of the
truck, and the girls stood waiting at the
counter.

"I'm not sure I actually *want* an ice cream cone now," Rachel whispered. "Should we go somewhere else?"

Kirsty was just about to agree when an extra paper hat on the counter, like the one Charlie was wearing, caught her eye. "Look!" she cried. "That hat! It's glowing!" Rachel's eyes widened in excitement. She carefully lifted the hat. Then she beamed as a tiny fairy fluttered out and landed on a stack of cones, her feet dangling over the edge. The fairy had long black hair and wore a pastel-striped

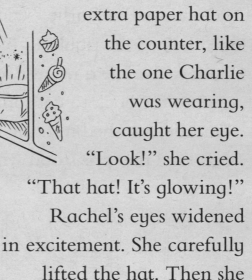

top, bright yellow
pants, and pink
sneakers. The stripes
on her shirt
reminded Rachel
of Raspberry
Ripple ice cream!

"Hello there,"
said the fairy in a
high, tinkling
voice. "I'm Esme
the Ice Cream Fairy!
We met earlier, in Fairyland."

"Hello again, Esme. I'm Kirsty, and
this is Rachel," Kirsty reminded her.

"And we're really glad to see you,"
Rachel said. She checked to make sure
that Charlie wasn't back before adding,

"The ice cream from this truck is *awful*!"

Esme nodded, looking serious. "It isn't
very good," she
agreed. "And
it's all because
Jack Frost took
my magic ice
cream cone
charm. I have
a feeling that
the goblins are
somewhere in
this market with my
charm. Would you mind helping me
look?"

"Mind? Not a bit!" Kirsty said eagerly.
"We'd love to!"

"Here we go," Charlie said just then,

reappearing with a large tub of chocolate ice cream in his arms. He opened the freezer and popped it inside. While his head was hidden in the freezer, Esme leaped off the cones and fluttered into Rachel's skirt pocket.

Charlie lifted his head, looking confused. "That's strange," he said. "All my ice cream seems to have melted. How could that have happened?"

"Oh, no," Rachel said.

"I'm sorry, girls," he went on. "Maybe

this freezer is broken. I'm afraid I'll have to close the truck while I investigate."

"Thanks anyway," Kirsty said. "I hope you can figure it out soon." She glanced at Rachel as they turned away. "I hope *we* can figure it out, really," she added in a whisper.

Esme poked her head out of Rachel's pocket, and the sun sparkled on her dark, wavy hair. "Let's keep a lookout for anything unusual," she said. "We have  to stop Jack Frost and the goblins, or there won't be any ice cream for Treat Day—the day after tomorrow!"

The girls wandered through the

market, watching carefully for anything strange going on. One lady selling jewelery had a hood hiding her face. Kirsty looked closely, wondering if she was a goblin in disguise. Then the lady gave her customer a beaming smile, and Kirsty glanced away. No—she definitely *wasn't* a goblin. No goblin was ever that nice and friendly!

Next was a booth selling wooden toys. Rachel narrowed her eyes suspiciously when she saw that the man there had a baseball cap pulled low over his face. Was *that* a goblin?

Then he lifted
his hat and
scratched his
head, and
Rachel saw
that his skin
was pink rather
than goblin-green.
No—he wasn't a goblin, either!

"Maybe the ice cream just melted in
the sun," Kirsty said doubtfully. "Maybe
Charlie's freezer really *did* break."

Esme shook her head. "No," she said.
"I'm sure I can sense goblins around here
somewhere. Let's keep looking."

"Hey, Kirsty," came a voice just then,
and the girls turned to see two boys
approaching.

"Hi, Liam! Hi, Jamal!" Kirsty said. "This is my friend Rachel. Liam and Jamal go to my school," she explained.

Rachel said hi, and then her gaze locked onto the boys' hands. Both of them were carrying enormous green ice cream cones!

Jamal licked his, a blissful expression on his face. "This is the best ice cream cone I've ever tasted," he said with a sigh. "The flavors sound really weird, but they taste amazing!"

Rachel and Kirsty exchanged a glance.

"Did you buy them from Charlie?" Kirsty asked, pointing at the truck behind them.

"No," Liam replied, "they're from that truck over there—the bright green one.

All of their ice cream is green, too!" Hidden in Rachel's pocket, Esme gave a squeak of excitement. Both girls knew why. The green ice cream truck must be connected with the goblins!

"Thanks," said Kirsty. "Come on,

Rachel. Let's go there right now!"

With a wave to the boys, the girls raced off. If they could find the goblins, maybe they could find Esme's magic charm, too!

# A Cool Pool?

There was a long line stretching back from the green ice cream truck, and the girls joined the end. Everyone walking away with their bright green ice cream cones was exclaiming how delicious they were.

"Look—we were right," whispered

Rachel. "There are goblins in the truck!"

Kirsty and Esme looked over. The three ice cream sellers in the truck were dressed in uniforms like Charlie's, except they were bright green. They wore hats over their eyes. But even the hats couldn't disguise what long noses they all had . . . and how green their skin was!

"One of them must have my magic ice cream cone charm!" said Esme. "Girls, should we find a quiet place so that I can turn you into fairies? Then we can fly into the truck for a closer look without anyone seeing us."

"Yes, please," Kirsty said at once.
Being a fairy was always so much fun!

Rachel and Kirsty
left the line and
hid behind a
truck selling
cups of tea
and coffee.
There, Esme
waved her wand
and murmured some
magic words. A swirl of
bright stars and sparkles flooded from
her wand and whirled around the girls.
They immediately shrank smaller and
smaller until they were the same size as
Esme! Then they fluttered off the ground
with their very own shimmering, gauzy
wings.

"Thank you!" Rachel cried, twirling
in midair.

"Let's investigate," Kirsty said,
zooming high. "Come on!"

The three fairies flew above the crowd
as they headed for the green ice cream

truck. The back door was
open, so they zipped
inside and hid on a
shelf behind a huge tub
of green ice cream.
Peeking out, they could
see the three goblins

working at the counter.

"There you go," said the first goblin to
a customer, handing over two cones of
green ice cream decorated with green
fudge sauce. "Who's next?"

"This is the best job ever," the second

goblin said. He was making an ice
cream sundae, decorated with green
whipped cream. He paused to squirt
whipped cream into his mouth. "Yum!"
he said happily.

"We shouldn't use all the ice cream,
remember," the third goblin said bossily.
"We have to keep enough for Jack Frost's
Candy Castle."

"That's right—he's going to fill his
swimming pool with ice cream!" the first
goblin said, adding green sprinkles to
another cone. "How cool is that?" He
chuckled suddenly. "Cool—ice cream.
Get it?"

The fairies exchanged glances as the
goblins laughed.

"I wouldn't want to swim in ice
cream," Rachel whispered,
shivering. "Think
how cold it
would be."

"And sticky,"
Kirsty said,
wrinkling her
nose.

Esme looked upset.
"Ice cream isn't meant for *swimming* in,"

she said. "It's for cones and sundaes and milkshakes. What is Jack Frost thinking?"

"It's such a waste, too," Rachel agreed. "Especially when the fairies need ice cream for Treat Day. We need to find your magic charm fast, and stop all this craziness!"

# Turning Green

While the girls were talking, the goblins had started bickering. "The ice cream pool should be Spinach Swirl flavor," the first goblin said.

"No way—Broccoli Chunk is the best," the second goblin argued, squirting more whipped cream into his mouth.

"You two don't know what you're talking about," the third added.

"Cabbage Surprise
is the tastiest.
Imagine
jumping off
the diving board
and landing
headfirst
in *that*!"

"Diving board?
There isn't going to be
a diving board," scoffed the first goblin.
"I heard Jack Frost was putting one of
those superfast water slides in the pool.
It's going to be awesome!"

While the goblins squabbled, Kirsty,
Rachel, and Esme began quietly
searching through the truck. It was
stocked with lots of different flavors of

ice cream (all green) plus green sprinkles,
green sauces, green cones, green
cherries, and green
chocolate flakes.
Searching
through
everything was
nerve-racking
—especially
since the
goblins were so close
and kept turning around
to use different toppings and
sauces! Both Kirsty and Rachel had
to move very quickly more than once
so that they wouldn't be spotted.

Unfortunately, after searching
high and low, there was no sign of

Esme's magic ice cream cone charm
anywhere.

"I don't understand," Esme sighed as
they fluttered back to the shelf. "We've
looked everywhere! Where could it be?"

"Maybe one of the
goblins is wearing
it on a chain
around his
neck," Kirsty
suggested. Each
fairy flew to a
different goblin,
perched lightly
on his shoulder, and peered carefully
down his collar. They didn't see any
chains, though.

"Do they have pockets on their

uniforms?" Esme wondered. "Maybe one goblin has the charm hidden in a pocket."

It took only a moment for them to realize that the goblins didn't have any pockets on their jackets, so the magic charm couldn't be there, either.

Just as they were starting to feel stumped, Rachel's eye was caught by the goblins' paper hats. She remembered how Esme had been hiding in one earlier. "Maybe the charm is underneath one of their hats," she whispered. "But which one?"

Kirsty thought for a moment. "I have an idea," she said with a smile. "Follow me."

Kirsty flitted out of the back door with Esme and Rachel close behind, and explained her plan.

"The goblins are arguing so much already, I bet we can persuade them to have a food fight with the ice cream.

And then their hats are sure to be knocked off!" she said.

"I love it," Esme said. "But how can we encourage them to have a food fight?"

Rachel grinned. "By starting one ourselves," she suggested. "Could you use your magic to disguise us as goblin ice cream sellers, Esme? We could set a very bad example for them. . . ."

Esme's eyes twinkled. "Perfect," she said. "I'll just get rid of this crowd of people first. I would hate for any of them to get splattered!"

Esme tapped herself lightly on the head

with her wand
and murmured
a magic spell.
Then she began
to speak, but
her words came
out much louder
than usual. In fact,
she sounded exactly
like a loudspeaker
announcement!

"Ladies and gentlemen," she boomed.
"I regret to inform you that the Bright
Green Ice Cream Machine has now run
out of ice cream, and we are no longer
able to serve you. We apologize for any
inconvenience."

A sigh of dismay went up from the

crowd that had gathered around the truck. The goblins were still arguing, and didn't even notice their line wandering away!

Esme tapped her head again, breaking the spell on her voice. "There—now for part two of the plan," she said with a mischievous smile. "Two new ice cream sellers!"

She waved her wand, and a flurry of magic sparkles flew around Kirsty and Rachel. The girls grew bigger and greener, with pointy noses and big ears.

Rachel giggled at the sight of her and
Kirsty. They looked just like the goblins,
and had trays of ice cream hanging
around their necks. "We definitely look
nicer as fairies than goblins!" she said.

"I don't feel very dainty anymore, with these enormous feet," Kirsty agreed with a grin. She adjusted her tray of ice cream. "But never mind. We have a plan to try out. Let's hope it works!"

## splat!

Rachel took a deep breath as she and
Kirsty walked out around the front of the
truck. She knew that Esme's magic
wouldn't last long. They only had a few
minutes before their goblin disguises
wore off. They had to get this right!

Kirsty gave Rachel a wink, then
launched right into their plan. "You did

it again, didn't you?" she said in a loud, angry voice. "I TOLD you not to keep eating the ice cream. We're supposed to be taking it back to Jack Frost, remember?"

"I know that!" Rachel snapped. "And it's not ME who's been eating the ice cream, anyway. It must be you!" With that, she grabbed a scoop of ice cream from a tub left on the counter by a lazy goblin.

The ice cream flew through the air, knocking Kirsty's hat off.

"How dare you?" Kirsty cried, pretending to be outraged. "Take THAT!" She grabbed a nearby stack of cones and threw them back at Rachel.

As she bent to pick up her hat, Kirsty saw the goblins' faces light up with glee. Goblins could never resist a fight! Within moments, they had all joined the food fight—hurling ice cream, sprinkles,

and cherries at one another. One goblin
even used the can of whipped cream like
a water pistol, squirting the other goblins
in the face.

Rachel and Kirsty grinned. Their plan
was working! They each grabbed more
ice cream and began hurling lumps of it
into the truck.

*Splat!* One lump knocked off the first goblin's paper hat . . . but nothing was hidden underneath.

*Splat!* Kirsty had to aim high since the next goblin was tall, but the gooey scoop she threw sent his hat flying, too. She held her breath as it fell . . . but his head was bare beneath it.

Now there was only one goblin left wearing a hat. Kirsty and Rachel both took careful aim. *Splat! Splat!* Kirsty's

scoop of ice cream just missed, hitting
him on the ear and sliding down
his neck. Rachel's scoop,
however, was a direct hit,
and sent his paper
hat flying!
Underneath was
a small pink and
gold ice cream cone
charm, sparkling as it
lay on the goblin's head!

"Quick, Esme!" whispered Rachel in
delight.

Hiding in Rachel's pocket, Esme had
seen everything. She darted out like a
bright ember of light, flying straight for
the magic charm.

Just as Esme was about to reach out
and grab it, one of the other goblins

noticed her. "Hey, watch out! There's a
sneaky fairy in here!" he cried, swatting
at Esme with his ice cream scoop.

"She's after the magic cone!" the tall
goblin realized. He snatched the charm
off the third goblin's head and dashed
out of the truck as fast as he could.

Rachel opened her mouth to shout
"After him!" but remembered at the last
second that she was still disguised as a
goblin. Instead, she cried, "Don't worry,
I'll catch that fairy!" and ran behind
Esme, who was already flying after the
tall goblin.

Kirsty joined her. "Come back here!"
she yelled. Really, both girls hoped Esme
would catch up with the tall goblin.
Unfortunately, he was a fast runner and
showed no sign of slowing down.

"He's getting away," Rachel realized
with a groan as they raced along behind
the goblin and Esme.

"And our plan had been working so
well!" Kirsty sighed. "Now what are we
going to do?"

# Trapped!

"The goblin's too fast! I don't think Esme can catch him," Rachel said. "Unless he ends up in a dead end somewhere. . . ."

Kirsty grinned. "Wouldn't it be awful if his goblin friends sent him the wrong way?" she said with a wink. "There's an alley just off the main road that's a dead end. Let's try to send him down there."

"Genius!" Rachel smiled, then called ahead to the goblin. "There's a shortcut on your left!" she yelled. "You can get away from the fairy if you go that way."

He glanced back, saw Rachel—still disguised as a goblin—and gave her a thumbs-up. Then he ducked down the alley, with Esme, Kirsty, and Rachel all following him.

Of course, the alley wasn't a shortcut at all— it ended in a high brick wall. There was no escape! The goblin spun around. "This isn't a shortcut!" he yelled. His eyes widened at the sight of Esme darting toward him. "Now what?"

"Throw the charm to me, I'll keep it safe!" Rachel called.

Thinking she was a goblin, the tall goblin did just that. Rachel deftly caught the charm and held it out on her palm for Esme.

The goblin's jaw dropped as Esme flew down to take it. In the next second, the girls' goblin disguises wore off.

"You tricked me!" the goblin wailed, stamping his foot. "No fair!" The other two goblins had caught up now, panting and clutching their sides. They groaned when they realized what had happened. "And we used up almost all the ice cream in our food fight," one of them complained nervously. "Jack Frost is going to be so angry!"

The goblins looked so worried, the girls felt a little sorry for them. "It's not your fault that Jack Frost is so greedy," Kirsty said.

"Nobody needs an ice cream swimming pool," Rachel added.

Esme smiled. "Do you think an ice cream *bath* would be OK, instead?" she asked, twirling her wand. Suddenly, a large white bathtub on wheels appeared . . . filled with glittering green ice cream!

The goblins looked much more cheerful. "Thank you," they said, and wheeled the bathtub away down the alley.

Esme fastened her magic charm bracelet around her wrist. A sudden bright flash of light sparked in the air. "There," she said happily. "Now ice cream everywhere should be super-tasty again."

Rachel grinned. "Well, there's only one way to find out," she said. "Come on, let's pay another visit to Charlie."

The three friends went back down the alley. To their delight, they saw that Charlie had opened his ice cream truck again and had a long line of customers waiting eagerly.

"Hooray!" Esme cheered at the sight. "Thank you both so much. I'd better go back to Fairyland now to work on my new flavors for Treat Day. Enjoy your ice cream!"

"I'm sure we will," Kirsty said. She and Rachel watched Esme fly away until she was just a tiny dot in the sky. Then she vanished! The girls joined Charlie's line.

After all that running, they felt awfully hungry!

It took a while for Rachel and Kirsty to reach the front of the line, but when it was finally their turn, they noticed two new flavors on the display board. "Ooh, Strawberry Sparkle sounds good," Kirsty said, opening her purse.

"And I'd like the Marshmallow Magic flavor, please," Rachel said.

Charlie smiled and handed over their ice cream cones. Just as he went to serve the next customer, a pinch of glittery sprinkles appeared on their ice cream, and the girls beamed. They knew the sprinkles were a gift from Esme. Fairy magic was so wonderful!

Rachel and Kirsty walked away, licking their ice cream. "*Mmm,*" Rachel

said. "Marshmallow
Magic is absolutely
delicious."

"So is Strawberry
Sparkle," Kirsty said
happily. Then she
remembered
something. "Oh —
and we still have
Aunt Helen's
surprise for us back
at home! I wonder what it is."

"One thing's for sure," Rachel said as
they walked along. "With all of these
Sugar and Spice Fairy adventures, we're
in for a tasty time!"

Rachel and Kirsty found Lisa and Esme's missing
magic charms. Now it's time for them to help

# Coco
### the Cupcake Fairy!

Join their next adventure in this
special sneak peek. . . .

# A Sweet Surprise

"This has been such an exciting day," said Rachel Walker, licking her Marshmallow Magic ice cream. "We've already been to Fairyland *and* helped two fairies get their magic charms back from Jack Frost."

Rachel and her best friend, Kirsty Tate, were walking home from the Wetherbury village square, where they had been looking around the market. Rachel was visiting Kirsty for spring break, and it looked like they were going to have an exciting week.

"The day's not over yet," added Kirsty, smiling. She paused to lick her Strawberry Sparkle ice cream, which was melting in the hazy afternoon sun and running over her fingers. "I have a feeling that now that magical things have *started* happening, they're going to *keep* happening!" she went on, licking her fingers one by one.

No one in the human world knew that the girls had been on many adventures in Fairyland. They were always excited to make new fairy friends and help outwit Jack Frost and his naughty goblins. That morning, Honey the Candy Fairy had visited them to ask for help again. This time, Jack Frost and his goblins had stolen the seven magic charms belonging to the Sugar and Spice Fairies. Without them, all of the candy and treats in both the human world and Fairyland were ruined!

"We've already rescued Lisa the Lollipop Fairy's magic lollipop charm and Esme the Ice Cream Fairy's magic ice cream cone charm," Rachel said, chewing on a deliciously sticky marshmallow. "But there are still five more charms to find."

"And if we don't find them fast, Fairyland's Treat Day will be ruined!" said Kirsty, biting her lip.

The day after tomorrow was Treat Day in Fairyland. King Oberon and

Queen Titania always gave a basket of special treats to each fairy to thank them for their hard work all year. But Jack Frost was using the Sugar and Spice Fairies' magic charms to get all the treats for himself. There weren't any left for the fairies! He was planning to build a giant Candy Castle, and he had given the magic charms to his goblins for safekeeping.

The goblins had come to the human world to find even *more* treats to steal for the Candy Castle. Rachel and Kirsty kept a careful lookout for the little green troublemakers as they walked past the village hall. They knew that goblins could pop up anywhere!

# RAINBOW magic™

# Which Magical Fairies Have You Met?

- ❑ The Rainbow Fairies
- ❑ The Weather Fairies
- ❑ The Jewel Fairies
- ❑ The Pet Fairies
- ❑ The Dance Fairies
- ❑ The Music Fairies
- ❑ The Sports Fairies
- ❑ The Party Fairies
- ❑ The Ocean Fairies
- ❑ The Night Fairies
- ❑ The Magical Animal Fairies
- ❑ The Princess Fairies
- ❑ The Superstar Fairies
- ❑ The Fashion Fairies
- ❑ The Sugar & Spice Fairies

**■ SCHOLASTIC**

Find all of your favorite fairy friends at
**scholastic.com/rainbowmagic**

# SPECIAL EDITION

# Which Magical Fairies Have You Met?

**3 stories in each one!**

- ☐ Joy the Summer Vacation Fairy
- ☐ Holly the Christmas Fairy
- ☐ Kylie the Carnival Fairy
- ☐ Stella the Star Fairy
- ☐ Shannon the Ocean Fairy
- ☐ Trixie the Halloween Fairy
- ☐ Gabriella the Snow Kingdom Fairy
- ☐ Juliet the Valentine Fairy
- ☐ Mia the Bridesmaid Fairy
- ☐ Flora the Dress-Up Fairy
- ☐ Paige the Christmas Play Fairy
- ☐ Emma the Easter Fairy
- ☐ Cara the Camp Fairy
- ☐ Destiny the Rock Star Fairy
- ☐ Belle the Birthday Fairy
- ☐ Olympia the Games Fairy
- ☐ Selena the Sleepover Fairy
- ☐ Cheryl the Christmas Tree Fairy
- ☐ Florence the Friendship Fairy
- ☐ Lindsay the Luck Fairy
- ☐ Brianna the Tooth Fairy
- ☐ Autumn the Falling Leaves Fairy
- ☐ Keira the Movie Star Fairy
- ☐ Addison the April Fool's Day Fairy

## 📖 SCHOLASTIC

Find all of your favorite fairy friends at
**scholastic.com/rainbowmagic**